Charlotte was a little lamb born in a Galloway spring.
She grew a fluffy, woolly fleece, the very warmest thing.

The rain could rain, the sleet could sleet,
the snow could snow and snow.
Charlotte's fleece would keep her snug
as she wandered to and fro.

Charlo Yarn

A Spin Scotland

To My Dad
Alan Grant
The ultimate super hero.

At last the ice all went away,
the grass begn to green.
The birds began to chirp and sing, and build their nests and preen.

Charlotte had a lovely time,
she ran and played all day.

Until the farmer's dog came by,
and made her run away.

He chased her down the hillside, along a stony track;
where the farmer took a hold of her and turned her on her back.

He let her go soon afterwards, and she trotted off, quite cross.
A chilly wind blew on her back,
her lovely fleece was lost!

What would the man do with her fleece?
Charlotte wasn't sure.
When he drove off, she followed him, across the lonely moor.

The wind was chill, poor Charlotte cold,
the moon was very bright.
She must find her fleece to keep her warm,
she shivered through the night.

She saw a man atop a plinth, upon his head, a bird.
He had an honest, sonsy face
but uttered not a word.

On and on she wandered, day and night and day.
The man was nowhere to be seen, her coat now far away.

Mountains, moorlands, forests, towns,
Charlotte searched them all.
She found the world was really big, and she felt really small.

What a lovely harbour!
Charlotte wondered at the view.
Had her fleece sailed far across the sea,
Away to places new?

The days went on from sun to rain
and back to sunshine bright.

Charlotte was determined
to make everything alright.

Then suddenly a flake of snow, white flakes began to fall.
Without a fleece what would she do?
She had no chance at all.

But Charlotte quickly realised that she couldn't feel the ice.
She was warm and snuggly; it felt really, really nice!

She turned her head around and saw her back was bare no more.
A lovely woolly fleece was there, thicker than before!

Now Charlotte's happy where she is, grazing in the sun.
Her fleece is shorn off every spring,
but she grows another one!

Shalla Gray lives in a wee village in rural Galloway with her partner and four children.
Charlotte's Woolly Yarn was Shalla's first published book; now reissued with extra verses as she had regretted missing out the towns of Dumfries and Kirkcudbright in the original version.
Shalla is pictured below, with her unicorn Jeff.

Also from Curly Tale Books

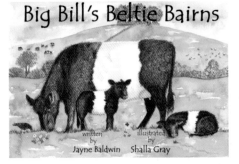

And coming soon...